FART MONSTER AND ME

For Jess — thanks for all your support and laughing at all my fart jokes (even when they weren't funny) — TM

For any kid who hasn't decided if they like reading yet — this is for you — MS

 The ABC 'Wave' device is a trademark of the Australian Broadcasting Corporation and is used under licence by HarperCollins*Publishers* Australia.

First published in Australia in 2018
by HarperCollins*Children'sBooks*
a division of HarperCollins*Publishers* Australia Pty Limited
ABN 36 009 913 517
harpercollins.com.au

HarperCollins*Publishers*
Level 13, 201 Elizabeth Street, Sydney NSW 2000, Australia
Unit D1, 63 Apollo Drive, Rosedale, Auckland 0632, New Zealand
A 53, Sector 57, Noida, UP, India
1 London Bridge Street, London SE1 9GF, United Kingdom
2 Bloor Street East, 20th floor, Toronto, Ontario M4W 1A8, Canada
195 Broadway, New York NY 10007, USA

A catalogue record for this book is available
from the National Library of Australia

ISBN 978 0 7333 3893 9

Cover design by Matt Stanton
Consultant editor: Louise Park
Typeset in Bembo Infant by Kirby Jones
Printed and bound in Australia by McPherson's Printing Group
The papers used by HarperCollins in the manufacture of this book are a natural, recyclable product made from wood grown in sustainable plantation forests. The fibre source and manufacturing processes meet recognised international environmental standards, and carry certification.

FART MONSTER AND ME

AND ME

The New School

TiM MiLLER + MATT STANTON

ABC
Books

PROLOGUE

Things you need to know about me:

My name is Ben Dugan.

I share my bedroom with a green fart monster.

He's been my friend ever since he crash-landed in my yard.

We do everything together.

I'm the only one who can see him.

I try to hide what my monster gets up to. If I can't hide it, I get **blamed** for it!

Mum and Dad have no idea what's going on. But they do know one thing: it's become much **smellier** since the fart monster moved in.

I sure hope the fart cloud doesn't spread. Or follow me to Stone Beach Primary for my first day at my new school …

CHAPTER 1

'Mum! I can't find my school bag,'
I called out.

'It's in one of the boxes!' Mum
yelled back. She was still looking
for her car keys downstairs.

I frowned. There were **loads**
of boxes in my new bedroom. My
school bag could be in any of them.

My family had just moved

to Stone Beach on the weekend.

Mum was starting a new job here.

It wasn't fair. I had to go to my

new school the very next day.

'Any idea which one it's in?'

I asked the fart monster.

He looked around the room.

'You didn't label the boxes like your

mum asked?'

'No ...'

A **cheeky** smile spread across the

fart monster's green face.

'At least help me find my bag,'
I said. I picked up a box and tipped
it over.

The fart monster was keen to
help. He tipped over another box.
It didn't have my school bag in it.

'You should open that box,'
the fart monster said. He pointed
to the biggest box in the room.

I peeled off the tape. A **terrible** smell hit me in the face. It had been stuck in the box for days.

'You trapped a fart in here!' I spluttered.

The fart monster was rolling on the floor laughing.

'Pull yourself together. Help me find my school bag.'

We opened box after box. All of my stuff was spread over the floor and bed. My school bag was in the last box we opened.

Mum stood at my door.

Her mouth was **wide open**.

I held up my school bag like

a prize. 'Found it.'

CHAPTER 2

'I don't get why Mum is so angry,'
I said to the fart monster as we
walked to the car. 'We found my
school bag.'

The fart monster shrugged.
'What will we do at school today?'
he asked.

I stared at him. 'Huh?'

'Stone Beach Primary. First day,'

the fart monster said.

'I thought you would stay at

home,' I replied.

'Why would I do that? Just

think how bad the smell would be.

Me, locked inside all day long?'

'Oh, I hadn't thought about that.
I guess we're going to Stone Beach
Primary then!'

We climbed into the back of
the car and put on our seatbelts.

Mum locked up the house, then
ran to us.

'I only just found my keys.
How did you get in the car, Ben?'

'It was unlocked.'

Mum shook her head and
mumbled something under her
breath. Then she said, 'We are going
to be so late.'

The fart monster let one rip in
the car. Mum sighed and turned on
the fan. The fart monster laughed.
I held on to my nose.

But what if he farted at school?

What would the other kids think?

What would they think of *me*?

I wasn't so sure about the fart

monster coming along now.

Would the kids at Stone Beach Primary be nice?

Would they like me?

What if they thought the farts were *mine*?

Mum turned on the blinker. We drove past my new school.

It was huge!

So many kids were walking through the gate. They were all talking. Already friends.

How would I fit in?

CHAPTER 3

Cars were lined up outside Stone Beach Primary. Mum pulled into the drop-off area.

'Are you keen for your first day?'

'Kind of.' *Only if no one farts in class*, I thought, hopping out of the car. The fart monster was right behind me.

'Okay, go to the school office first. And have a great day! Dad will pick you up at three.'

We waved goodbye to Mum. Tears pooled in her eyes.

'Mums cry at odd things,' the fart monster said.

Mum opened all the windows before driving off.

I looked around. 'How am I going to find the office? The school is even bigger than I thought! And there aren't any signs to help me.'

The fart monster pointed to

a boy. 'Just ask him where it is.

He seems like a nice guy.'

I walked over to the boy. 'Hi.'

'Hello,' the boy replied.

'I'm new here. Can you tell me where the office is?'

'Yeah, it's over there.' The boy pointed to a blue building, then smiled at me.

'Thanks,' I said, dragging the fart monster along with me.

'See, that wasn't so bad,' the fart monster said.

'I've made a friend!' I said.

The fart monster **frowned**.

'Don't get ahead of yourself.'

CHAPTER 4

Lots of adults were in the office.

They all looked super busy.

The person behind the front desk

looked up.

'You must be Ben. I'm Miss

Summers.'

'Hi,' I said with a small wave.

'We're so happy that you're

joining us at Stone Beach.

Your parents couldn't come with

you this morning?'

'Dad had to start early. Mum

dropped me off at the gate. She was

running late for work.'

'So, you made it here on your own. That's **great!**' she said.

'Hey, I helped too!' the fart monster said. He patted me on the back.

Miss Summers looked down at her desk. 'The class lists are here somewhere.'

I leant towards the fart monster. 'No one else can see you, remember?' I mumbled.

'True,' he said, nodding.

'Ah, here they are,' she said.

'So, Ben, you are going to be in Mr Bendentoot's class.'

'Bendentoot! He must **love** fart jokes,' the fart monster said.

We both giggled.

Miss Summers smiled. 'Just sit over there for a bit, Ben. I'll walk you to your class soon.'

CHAPTER 5

Miss Summers and I stepped into Mr Bendentoot's classroom. Twenty-five pairs of eyes stared at me.

There was no way on earth they wouldn't smell the fart monster. He was already eating snacks from my school bag.

He'd be letting off huge, smelly
farts soon enough!

'Hello, everyone,' said
Miss Summers. 'I'd like you all
to meet Ben Dugan. It's his first
day at Stone Beach Primary.
I know you will all make him
feel welcome.'

'Hello, Ben,' the entire class
replied.

'Hey,' I said softly.

The fart monster was waving at
the class with both hands.

'Ben, why don't you tell us a little about yourself?' Mr Bendentoot asked.

The fart monster turned towards me. 'Tell them about me! Tell them about the yellow gas cloud! Tell them where I came from!'

I turned away from the fart monster and said, 'Ummmm. Well, what would you like to know?'

'Anything you like, Ben,' Mr Bendentoot replied.

I stared at my feet for a moment. 'Umm … pull my finger?'

The class burst into laughter.

Mr Bendentoot did his best to hide his smile. 'Bit of a joke teller, are you?'

I shrugged.

'Why don't you take a seat, Ben. Then we'll start the class.'

I went to the spare desk by the window. The fart monster sat in the seat beside me.

'Ben,' he mumbled in my ear. 'I've got a big one on the way.'

Oh no!

CHAPTER 6

The bell rang for lunch. I hung back until everyone else had left the classroom. 'Mr Bendentoot, can you please tell me where the canteen is?'

Mum had given me some money for lunch. We still hadn't found my lunch box.

Another student raced back into the room. Mr Bendentoot stopped her.

'Ben, this is Laura. Laura, can you show Ben where the canteen is?'

'Sure! Ben, come with me.'

I smiled and followed Laura out of the room. The fart monster was two steps behind me. His gas cloud was two steps behind him.

'The canteen food is okay,' Laura said. 'Do you know what you want to get?'

The fart monster laughed. 'You should get baked beans. Or cabbage. Or fried eggs. Yum.'

'No idea,' I told Laura. 'Is there a menu?'

She laughed. 'It's not a five-star
cafe.'

'As long as there isn't any
cabbage ...'

Laura frowned. 'There's no
cabbage, but they have wraps and
fruit and choc milk?'

'Uh-oh,' I said, looking at the canteen.

The fart monster had run ahead. He was standing at the end of the big line. He bent over and his butt rumbled. The gas cloud sent everyone running. They ran away as fast as they could.

'Right,' the fart monster said to me. 'So, what are we going to buy?'

CHAPTER 7

I should never have let the

fart monster order lunch.

Worst. Mistake. EVER!

Back in class, I could hear his

tummy rumbling. No! The fart

monster couldn't fart in class.

Not on my first day!

If he farted, I'd get the blame!

And then I'd **never** make any friends.

Mr Bendentoot told the class to form into small groups. 'We're going to do art,' he said.

I bit my lip. The only person I knew was Laura. She was already sitting with a group of friends.

Panic struck me. Boy with one eyebrow. Girl with scrunchie. I knew no one!

The fart monster pointed to a group with only three kids.

He moved to join them. He squeezed

his butt cheeks together as he

walked. He was SO going to fart

when he got there.

I took a deep breath before I joined them. It might be my last chance for fresh air.

'Hey, Ben. I'm Sam. This is Dave and Chris.'

I sat down. 'Hi, guys.'

Mr Bendentoot put a vase of flowers on each group's table. 'Today we are going to draw these.'

The fart monster's belly rumbled again and he grinned. I twisted in my seat. I knew what was coming. There was a **rumble**.

There were lots of **rumbles**.

And then …

It was silent. But it was

deadly.

Sam's, Dave's and Chris's eyes watered. They looked like they might chuck. Even I thought I was going to be sick.

'Did something die?' Chris asked.

'Sir,' Dave called out. 'Someone farted!'

'**Ewww!** We need to get out of here,' a kid cried.

'Whoever smelt it, dealt it,' I said.

'It was Ben! Whoever denied it, supplied it!' Sam chanted.

I went red. My dad hadn't taught me that one!

The fart monster was rolling around laughing.

CHAPTER 8

Finally, the last bell rang and school was over. I was so tired. In the end, I couldn't even say it wasn't me any more. The whole class blamed me for the massive, deadly fart.

One kid named Steve had to open all the windows.

Some of the kids waved books like fans.

Mr Bendentoot got out the vacuum cleaner. He fixed the settings to blow air. Then he used it to blow the smell outside.

'Did you have to eat eggs?'
I asked the fart monster as I put
on my school bag.

He grinned. 'They had them at
the canteen!'

'That doesn't mean you had to
order them. I really didn't need you
farting. Not on our first day.'

'I told you fart jokes were a great
way to make new friends.'

'Doing farts and telling fart jokes
are NOT the same,' I said. 'I made
no new friends today. Not even one.'

As we made our way to the gate, Chris and Sam ran past.

'**Smell you later**, Ben!' Chris yelled.

'Gotta get **downwind** before you go off again,' Sam called.

The fart monster waved goodbye.

I groaned. People were always going to think it was me.

At the gate, I looked for my dad's car. It was new and really cool. The roof comes down, so there's plenty of open air.

No room for trapped farts.

'Hey, Ben.'

'Oh, hi, Laura.'

'Good work today. No one's ever asked Mr Bendentoot to pull their finger before.'

'Thanks, I think.'

Laura laughed. 'See you tomorrow.'

I waved as Laura got into the back of her mum's car.

'Ben, over here!' Dad called.

I raced over and hopped into his car. Dad ruffled my hair.

The fart monster climbed over the back door. He fell face first onto the seat.

'How was your first day, champ? Did you make any new friends?'

'Oh, I **blew** them away, Dad.'

The End

Want more farts?
Go back to where it all began ...

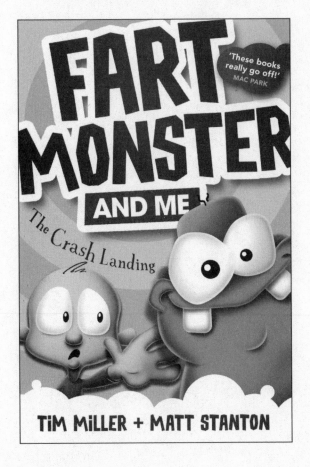